MUSIC FROM THE SKY

In loving memory of
Grampa Elmer Jones and
Grampa Hubert Francis – D G

Over my head, I hear music in the air
— TRADITIONAL SPIRITUAL

In memory of my mother – S T

Text copyright © 2001 by C. Denise Gillard
Illustrations copyright © 2001 by Stephen Taylor

Groundwood Books / Douglas & McIntyre
720 Bathurst Street, Suite 500, Toronto, Ontario M5S 2R4

Distributed in the USA by Publishers Group West
1700 Fourth Street, Berkeley, CA 94710

We acknowledge the financial support of the Canada Council for the Arts, the Ontario Arts Council and the Government of Canada through the Book Publishing Industry Development Program for our publishing activities.

Canadian Cataloguing in Publication Data

Gillard, Denise, 1961-
Music from the sky
"A Groundwood book".
ISBN 0-88899-311-0
I. Taylor, Stephen, 1964- . II. Title.
PS8563.I4824M87 2001   jC813'.6   C00-932396-1
PZ7.G54Mu 2001

Printed and bound in China by Everbest Printing Co. Ltd.

MUSIC FROM THE SKY

DENISE GILLARD

PICTURES BY

STEPHEN TAYLOR

A GROUNDWOOD BOOK

DOUGLAS & McINTYRE

VANCOUVER / TORONTO / BUFFALO

*E*ARLY morning.
Shhh!
No one is up but Grampa and me.
I sneak down the stairs.
Creak, creak, creak.

"Come on, girl. Put on your boots."

"Where are we going, Gramps?"

"Going to make a flute," he says.

"You can't make a flute! I've been to a concert. I've seen the long, shiny silver flute sounding so pretty, just like music from the sky. You can't make a flute, can you, Gramps?"

Grampa makes a funny face at me.
He says I'm a real crazy girl.

"Music from the sky? When did you
ever hear any music from the sky?" he
asks.

I heard the music one day when I was looking up at the clouds blowing by. Big fluffy, puffy clouds that looked like bears and boats and then…

"I heard it! Music from the sky! Gramps, if you close your eyes real tight and listen, I bet you could hear it, too!"

Gramps smiles at me. He says I'm a
wonder. Then, just like that he's ready to
go. "Are you coming?" he asks.
"Yes, I'm coming to make a flute!"

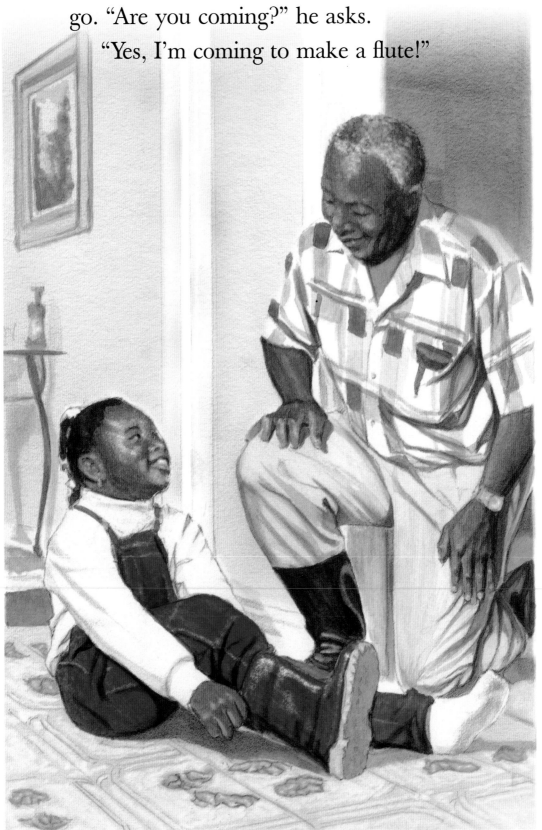

Squish, squish, squish.

Good thing we have our boots on. It gets awfully muddy out here on the marsh. Perfect place for getting making stuff says Grampa.

"Oh, Grampa. You can't really make a flute. You're just teasing."

My grandfather's eyes twinkle when he laughs at me.

He thinks I'm too small to know what
a flute looks like. I remember going to a
concert with my mom. After the concert,
all the children had to line up so we could
try out the instruments.

I was the first kid in line. I took a deep
breath and blew into the flute. All I heard
was air! It takes lots of practice to make
those sweet sounds. I bet if I get the
chance, I'll be a great musician some day.

"Hey, dreamer," calls Gramps.
"Let's get busy."

We look at tree branches.
Can't be too fat, too dry or too rough.
We search.

Finally! We find the right branch.

My grandfather lets me carry the branch home. I have to be very careful. This isn't just any ordinary stick, you know.

Back at the house, Grampa sits in his
favorite chair. He takes out his long, shiny
silver knife and whittles away at the
branch. He whittles the wood and soon…

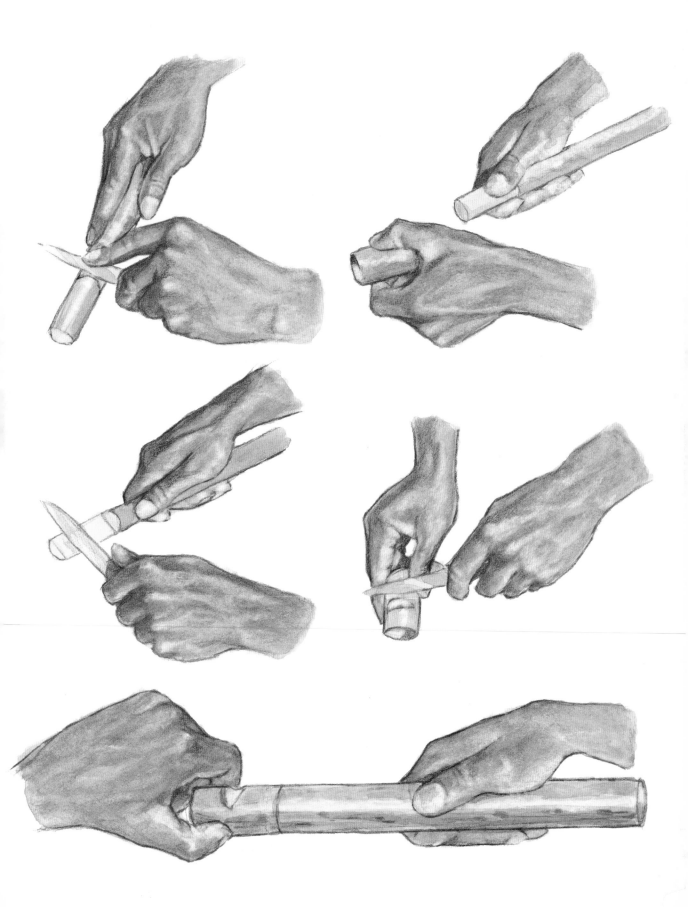

"It's a flute!"

I blow into it.
What a sound!

Now I'm making music…
Sounding so pretty…
Just like music from the sky.